CONTROL OF CLIMATE

MIGUEL ÁNGEL COLMENERO MARTÍN

Author: Miguel Ángel Colmenero
Martín Cover design: The author of the
book 1st edition
2024

To all the people who have crossed my path, to those whose challenges taught me valuable , and to those who, with their support and affection, gave me the strength lessonsto move forward. To all of you, without exception, I thank you for being part of my story, each of you, in some way, have contributed to the person I am today.

Miguel Ángel Colmenero Martín, born in Zamora, is a professional with an extensive background who, after more than twenty years of service as a civil servant, experienced a significant change in his career.

In 2013, after moving to a special administrative status, she had the opportunity to train in various areas of interest, which allowed her to delve into such relevant topics as mindfulness, disorders in childhood, adolescence and old age, learning difficulties, eating disorders in adolescence and sexual , disordersamong others. This stage of training represented a turning point in her life, as it allowed her to expand her perspective and explore new ways of helping others.

In 2020, after confinement, he decided to embark on the project of writing his first book, entitled "Manual of Positivism". This work is a compilation of inspirational and positive reflections both by himself and other thinkers, with the aim of offering tools and resources to help foster an optimistic mindset.

However, after deep reflection, Michelangelo decided not to publish that book, considering that its purpose was not to not only the publication, but the personal process of writing down his ideas.

In 2024, with the same passion and dedication that drove him to write his first project, he wrote and published his second book: Addicted to gambling or addicted to money? A literary work, which is presented as an autobiographical narrative through a dialogue with a friend, but is actually inspired by the real experiences of people he met throughout his life, through which he explored the complex relationships that exist between addiction to gambling and addiction to money, issues of growing relevance in today's society.

Now with this story, El control del clima, Miguel Ángel reaffirms his commitment to share his vision and knowledge about issues that, although often invisible, have a profound impact on people's lives. Through his words, he seeks to generate a deep reflection on the forces that operate in the shadows, those that try to shape our destiny and that of future generations.

In a world where the power of elites is deployed with the intention of manipulating and controlling every aspect of our existence, Michelangelo invites to reflection and collective awakening.

This story, although written as a novel of anticipation, is actually a denunciation and an urgent call to action. It reminds us that, if we do not become aware of the threats to our freedom and our environment, the future we will face could be a scenario of oppression and hopelessness, from which it would be almost impossible to escape.

Introduction

For decades, the world has witnessed extreme weather phenomena, but what few know is that not all of these events are the product of nature. In the shadows, globalist elites have played and continue to play with the climate, using advanced technology to manipulate it at will. Their purpose is none other than absolute control, to control resources, nations, and ultimately, every human being on the planet.

But in the midst of it all, a resistance , has emergeda group of rebellious people willing to challenge those who believe they have the power to decide the future of the Earth and, social networks mainly, have begun to inform others about the existence of climate control systems. Their fight is not only for survival, but for freedom and justice, to return the planet to its natural course and restore the lost balance.

Chapter 1. The Weather as a Weapon: The Hidden .Secret

Weather modification had been a top-secret project for decades, but global geopolitics began to change when the first signs of its destructive effects became visible.

Some people in different parts of the world began to notice unusual patterns in weather phenomena. Affordable weather manipulation technologies such as cloud seeding and chemicals in the atmosphere were secretly used to alter rainfall, winds and, worse, to cause droughts, storms and extreme temperatures in strategic locations.

What was once considered a conspiracy theory was in fact a global military and economic project. The elites knew that the climate was the most powerful weapon at their disposal. If they could control the climate, they could control the world.

Chapter 2. The Business of Chaos: Power and Climate.

Large corporations and governments were the real beneficiaries of climate change.

While people suffered the consequences of extreme droughts, uncontrolled forest fires and devastating hurricanes, a few entities, with connections at all levels of power, reaped the fruits of their destruction.planned

Changes in climate served several purposes, stripping nations of their natural , resourcesmoving populations to areas that could be more easily controlled, and establishing catastrophe markets.

Every natural disaster, whether it was a heat wave or a cold drop, represented a human cost, but it became an economic opportunity for those who had the power to modify the weather.

Big energy companies, firms environmental engineering and agribusiness multinationals became the new power players. They used climate chaos to restructure the world, displacing thousands of people from their homes.

people and buying land at low prices, .while the countries simply watched helplessly

Chapter 3. Manipulated : ClimateThe New Order of Power.

As climatic alterations intensified, began more drastic . changes to be seenAreas that had been fertile and productive became desertsbarren . Chemicals in the atmosphere caused changes in rainfall and weather patterns. As storms became more destructive and droughts lengthened, it became clear that something was not natural. Chemtrails, traces of chemicals in the air, were seen in skies around the world.

The turn to climate control was not just a matter of changing the seasons. The great elites used these phenomena to push the world in a specific direction. Through disasters, globalist elites could redistribute resources, move large populations and create a new world order where control of infrastructure and natural resources was in the hands of large corporations.

Chapter 4. The Business of Climate: Water, Food and Power.

Climate manipulation not only altered the ecological balance of the planet, but also irreversibly transformed the global economic structure.

Areas that once depended on regular rainfall for agriculture began to face prolonged droughts. Over time, large water corporations positioned themselves as the new owners of the most valuable resource on the planet.

Access to water became an exclusive luxury for those who could pay for it. Meanwhile, agricultural multinationals took advantage of climate disruptions to reconfigure access to arable land and make extraordinary profits at the expense of millions of people who saw their land dry up or be flooded.

Food production also became a field dominated by a few industry giants.

Areas where rains were forced to fall, through weather modification techniques, created secondary markets for agricultural products.

But this supply was not accessible to all, high price policies increased hunger in the most affected regions, while corporations profited at the cost of so much suffering.

Chapter 5. Flood and Chaos: Tragedy and Manipulation.

In a coastal area of Spain, devastated by a great flood, the shortage of everything was alarming.

Volunteers played a crucial , roletheir involvement was fundamental both in the emergency work and insubsequent recovery of the affected areas. However, the management of both the national and regional governments was a real disaster. Faced with the magnitude of the damage caused by the fall of 800 liters of water per square meter, the central government was not at all visible or involved in the first moments of the crisis caused, unlike the immediate response it had when a few months earlier there was an earthquake in a neighboring country.

Undoubtedly there was a before and after this tragedy, and more, when it was proven, that a series broadcasted on a platform controlled by the elites who use the woke ,movements had predicted such a catastrophe, thousands of people who lost everything, family members, houses, businesses, land, vehicles...

Chapter 6. The Geoengineering of Dispossession.

Coastal , citiespreviously protected by natural , began to see flooding not only as a natural phenomenon, but as a planned effect. According to leaked documents, certain sectors of geoengineering used increased rainfall to flood specific areas in order to generate chaos, barrierswhile creating new reconstruction opportunities for big business. Weather maps showed specific areas of forced flooding, where the resources natural and land now available were quickly acquired by powerful conglomerates.

Through rainfall manipulation and technologiesstorm detour , corrupt governments and corporations were able to direct water to previously unexplored areas, ensuring that the most fertile and resource-rich areas were completely modified. Populations were forced to abandon their homes, and the control over the resources of these lands was secured by the oligarchs.

Chapter 7. The End of Nations.

As climate manipulation reached new levels of sophistication, national governments began to lose their ability to manage the crises that confronted them. Large technology corporations and energy companies began to play a much larger role in resource management and global policy, often superseding the authority of local and governments.national

The old political systems began to crumble, and the structures power that once defined the boundaries of nations dissolved into a sea of global corporations making economic and political decisions on behalf of their own interests. Climate intervention policies that were initially used as a means to protect the environment became an excuse to further centralize power. were establishedNew zones of influence , where corporations dictated the rules, and governments were unable to challenge their decisions.

The planet was no longer divided into sovereign nations, but into territories controlled by corporate conglomerates, each with its own agenda to control climate and resources.

Chapter 8. Climate and Control: The New Corporate .Order

In a conference room, executives of large multinationals were discussing the next steps in their plan to consolidate global governance.

A hologram showed the areas of the planet most affected by recent weather disasters, with data on droughts, fires and storms becoming increasingly predictable.

"Nations no longer have power. We are the future," said one of the leaders of a multinational energy corporation. "We have the resources, the technology and the control. Single government is not just a possibility, it is a necessity, and if it means we continue to manage the 'so-called climate crisis' in a way that benefits us, we will."
His voice echoed through the room, filled with managers and experts who nodded , as if what he was proposing was a

universally accepted truth. No one dared to question the corporation's plan.

Natural disasters, provoked or amplified, served as a pretext for multinationals to take absolute control of resources.

The power of international banks and energy corporations was no longer limited to financial control, but now extended to climate management, where monopoly over natural resources was the key to dominating the future.

Climate change was, in fact, the vehicle for this New World Order.

Chapter 9. The Collapse of the Frontiers.

The world watched in amazement as the borders of nations fell away in the face of increasing centralization of power. The creation of a global government was the culmination of decades of manipulation and social engineering.

Agreements between governments and corporations were sealed in the dark, leaving humanity in a state of total dependence. Every natural disaster was predicted, every drought, every storm, every heat wave, aligned perfectly with the needs of corporations.

The collapse of state structures allowed the single government to carry out a series of covert reforms that were presented as urgent measures for the salvation of the planet.

The laws that once regulated everything were replaced by global norms that guaranteed great elites absolute control of the markets.

Large corporations, under the guise of protecting the planet, dictated the policies to be followed.

Chapter 10. The Age of Global Government and Despair.

The population, disoriented and terrified by the continuous climatic disasters, began to accept a single authority. The laws that once governed nations no longer held sway; citizens were now subject to the interests of an economic and political system that no longer bore any relation to traditional structures.

Each country was now just an administrative region within a global system where the most important decisions were made by the managers who controlled the large companies.

The world that emerged from this chaos was a highly controlled . In cities, environmental monitoring technologies and surveillance networks expanded with the justification of protecting humanity from disasterssocietyclimate .

Every step, every movement, every consumption of resources was now recorded and regulated by the new global government.

Climate , fearperpetrated by years of manipulation, had allowed the elites to implement a system of control.total

Ordinary people, unable to question the official , lived in constant fear of the next catastrophe.narrativesclimate

Storms, extreme heat, wildfires and droughts were all factors that fueled despair.

of the world, which made it the population to accept easier for absolute control.

The production and distribution of food and water were managed by these gigantic conglomerates, and those who disobeyed the new laws or attempted to access resources outside the circuits established were persecuted and severely punished.

Chapter 11. Shadow .Resistance

Despite the advances in climate manipulation and the power of the elites, a small group of individuals began to resist. They began to uncover the real agenda behind climate disasters.

They had gained access to documents and images that confirmed the existence ofa global weather orchestrated by those damn corporations, in order to make profits and consolidate power under a system.modification plan single

This small group of people decided to risk everything to alert the world. They used communication channels, social networks and anonymous websites to spread the truth. They knew that in doing so, they were jeopardizing their reputation and perhaps something else, but the need to expose reality overcame their fears.

They started sharing videos of chemtrails, those commercial aircraft and military planes that are involved in dispersing chemicals, that was evidence climate geoengineering and creating controlled weather phenomena.

They exposed how the elites, under the guise of saving the planet from climate catastrophe, had been creating and manipulating disasters, pushing humanity towards a single government that controlled all aspects of life.human

Their publications went viral, but they also faced censorship and criticism from the subsidized disinformation media, and repression from those who were still asleep and by those in control.

Chapter 12. Exposing the Climate .Conspiracy

One night, in a live broadcast watched by thousands of people, a courageous ex-pilot of the geoengineering industry revealed secret details of the weather modification programs. He showed graphs, maps and recordings of scientific tests demonstrating how rainfall was being altered and storms artificially steered. "Climate change is not an accident," he said, "it is the result of planned intervention. And what we have now is a world controlled by those who created the problem, to make us believe they have the solution."

The resistance had begun, and many people could no longer ignore the truth.

As resistance grew, corporate control was further consolidated. However, the revelation of climate manipulation had sown some seeds of distrust.

A growing number of people began to question the system and demand accountability. How is this possible?

Why was the climate being manipulated on such a scale?

The days were lengthening as humanity lived under the control of the new global structures. Although the New World Order was more present than ever and the large corporations and their tentacles of influence were felt in every corner of the planet, resistance was beginning to organize.

The echo of a change, though distant, resounded louder.

In remote cities and rural areas, small groups of individuals began to understand that the future of humanity was in their hands. They already knew that climate disasters were no accident, and that behind every storm or drought there was a strategy designed to keep the population under control. And they joined the fight, looking for ways to dismantle the system that had upset the balance of the planet.
Information about weather manipulation was beginning to leak out and more, and the resistance was nurtured by others

many pieces of evidence that citizens had collected over the years.

It was chilling to learn that even the last pandemic was created intentionally. According to the official version given by all the governments of the world to the citizens, the virus had accidentally come out of a laboratory in Wuhan (China), and according to the information of the resistance, the virus had been artificially modified, a fact that was omitted by the subsidized media working for the elites, since the idea was to use it as an experiment of global control, and it worked out well, because .billions of humans around the world took the vaccines, with the consequences that this entailed In addition to altering the DNA of the people who received , they themcould have very serious side effects on health in the medium term.

There is even evidence that these vaccines were used to inject microchips or tracking devices to monitor the population.

It was clear that the pandemic was used as an excuse to implement a "New World Order."

The global government, for its part, was stepping up surveillance measures, knowing that dissent was growing everywhere. Atmospheric control centers were more advanced than ever, and climate monitoring was done in real time, allowing elites to adjust the climate to suit their own damned agenda. Meanwhile, the multinationals that dominated the natural resource markets were expanding at dizzying rates, taking more and more territory and leaving behind a trail of misery and despair.

Chapter 13. Agenda 2030: Creating a New World.

At a meeting that had been scheduled for several months, several groups of people showed up to map out a plan.

There were activists, former climate , scientistsjournalists and technology experts. They knew each other and had too many differences, but the situation required that these be overcome to achieve a single goal: to dismantle climate manipulation .and continue to expose the lies of the elites

One of those present, who had worked for years on secret geoengineering projects, began to explain what he had discovered, which was why he decided to join the resistance.

"What we have done has not only altered the climate, but we have created artificial ecosystems. I can show you how we generated hurricanes, how we dried up entire forests and how we created desert storms. In fact, we recently created an extratropical cyclone that transformed the arid landscape of the Sahara desert; creating several lakes. The rainfall that fell in a few days was the equivalent of a year in that area. The whole world is being driven by what they call "Agenda 2030", and what it really hides behind it is a false ecological discourse", he said, while displaying classified documents on climate .manipulation

The place, filled with people who had been mostly skeptical up to that point, now listened in silence. The data were irrefutable. Climate manipulation was not only for resource ; it controlwas also a tool to create a new era of slaveryglobal .

Chapter 14. The Great Replacement.

As the resistance succeeded in exposing the truth, the effects of climate manipulation became even more destructive.

Over the years, so-called climate change had caused massive population displacements, water wars and the collapse of entire economies.

In addition, the elites also did business with the now called migrants, as they helped them through the mafias to move mainly to the old continent.

The population of the African continent were the chosen ones for the "Great Replacement", which they helped with all available means at their disposal, which were many, to replace the native populations of Europe with others of African origin, destabilizing the continent, generating social and economic tensions, in addition the displaced became a cheap labor force, available for the industries operating under the umbrella of the new world government.

Chapter 15. The Global .Awakening

The small groups that had been fighting in the shadows for the truth began to find allies in unexpected places, all driven by the same desire, to rid the world of the psychopaths that dominated it. They continued to spread whatever information they could get their hands on. The alternative media, which had been their only channel, were now stronger than ever.

Across the globe, protests and demonstrations began to grow.

The future, for many, was still in their hands and they began to mobilize to recover their lands, defend their resources and demand the fall of the "New World Order" that had been imposed without their consent.

The fear that had been sown in the population with the climate disasters began to dissipate slowly and thousands of people rose up against the system of global oppression.

Local governments that still maintained some degree of autonomy, and although they were of different political ,parties began to protest against the government's directivesglobal .

They knew they were facing a system that was very prepared to repress any attempt at rebellion, but the first signs of organized disobedience began to .surface

Acts of resistance were not only limited to peaceful marches or street protests. There were direct actions, sabotage of geoengineering facilities, attacks on control centers climate and destruction of equipment used to disperse chemicals into the atmosphere.

Although resistance seemed to be gaining strength, the elites' international allies had already begun to implement solutions they believed to be definitive.

New control technologies were beginning to come into operation, and a more advanced system of biotechnological surveillance was announced that would monitor not only every aspect of human life such as food or health; the new systems would even control emotion and .thought

It was a totalitarian system, backed by artificial intelligence and advanced , biometricswhich ensured that the planet would not fall back into the hands of those who opposed total control.

However, most of the resistance preferred to die fighting than to live under the control of the elites.

In their last acts, they made public a new revelation, the chemicals used in geoengineering not only altered the climate, but also modified DNAhuman , creating beings that would be easier to control.

Now everything was much more .understandable

This shocking information spread around the world and created an even greater wave of revolt due to the indignation of the population.

With the world in the greatest chaos it had ever known, the mass awakening began to bear fruit and although the global powers still maintained an iron grip on resources, the people had become aware of their power.

Chapter 16. Resistance Against Total .Control

What seemed almost impossible years ago began to become a reality, .the global elite began to show signs of vulnerability Measures of repression and control intensified, but so did the strength of those fighting back. Artificial intelligence systems used to control the population, from surveillance drones to weather observation satellites, began to be hacked and disabled by cyberactivist groups.

Corporations that had managed geoengineering projects for decades saw all their darkest secrets leak out. Classified documents appeared regularly on independent websites, revealing not only climate manipulations, but also connections to military and experimental projects that sought to alter the geography of the planet for the exclusive benefit of the elites.

Meanwhile, the provoked climate change continued its devastating course, but with one fundamental difference, now almost everyone knew the truth.

Civil disobedience was expanding and people were beginning to challenge globalist . security forcesPeople took to the , demanding a ban on geoengineering and an end to climate manipulation projects. Local cooperatives were formed to supply, autonomously, the rural communities farthest from the control of large corporations. They began to regain control of their agricultural lands and water sources.

However, the elites were unwillingto lose power without a last stand. They used new tactics of repression, with directed-energy weapons to neutralize protests, barium chloride to keep crowds drowsy and under control, and implementing high-security concentration camps for those deemed threats to global stability.

Chapter 17. The Last Battle.

A summit of the most influential figures in global government, the members of Councilthe Global , met to discuss how to neutralize the growing threat. The idea was clear, total destruction of any attempt at revolt and extermination of those who possessed critical information.Climate Control

The Global Council leader spoke softly, referring to the imminent danger of the activists, "We know they have the capacity to take down our targets, but we are not going to let . It is time to take extreme measures.them

The rest of the members were silent, accepting the implications of his words. They could not turn back. The climate control technology had been designed to ensure their power, and the mass awakening was destroying that blueprint for their future.

The battle was being fought on two fronts: On the one hand, direct resistance actions were intensifying. On the other hand, the elites were taking desperate measures, using the technologymost advanced mind , control through the manipulation of brain waves, they tried to neutralize the most prominent leaders of the movement.

The latest confrontation took place in the Serrania de Ronda, where the global corporations had their base of operations. Former B.O.E.L. legionnaires, members of the resistance, had infiltrated several key points, and organized a series of coordinated attacks. The forces of the new order responded with brutality, but the ex-military men, who were well trained and fought with passion, did not stop.

Chapter 18. The Rebirth of Humanity.

The gigantic centers of climate control were beginning to fall and it was noticeable. The global system of manipulation and subjugation was slowly . fragmentingHowever, the struggle was not over. The global elite had not completely disappeared; although they had retreated to their safe havens and strongholds, their influence had not disappeared. Now, however, they did not have absolute control of the planet.

The "New World Order" had left a mark.deep Millions of people were still struggling with the aftereffects of the climate manipulation that had altered both their homes and their lives, with land destroyed by years of dispersed chemicals and artificial modification of ecosystems.

For the resistance, the rehabilitation of these ecosystems was one of their main objectives, but they also focused on restoring food sovereignty and water resources.

Regaining control over water, air and land was essential to achieve the autonomy that the globalist system had destroyed.

Large cities, teeming with people displaced man-made climate catastrophes, were beginning to see the light at the end of the tunnel and some of these 15-minute cities were beginning to transform into places of resistance.

Although recovery had begun, the challenges were immense.

Prolonged droughts, natural disasters caused by geoengineering experiments, and the slow regeneration of the environment required an enormous amountof joint effort and work.
In many places, scientists who had been displaced by the

or silenced by global corporations became the new leaders of reconstruction. Thanks to their knowledge, natural habitat restoration methods would be implemented that would be fundamental to partially reverse the damage caused.

But the globalist elites, now mostly in hiding, tried to manipulate the population with the last shreds of power they had. Their new attempts to create a digital economy controlled by virtual currencies and surveillance networks failed to meet opposition.tenacious

Local governments, with the support of the resistance, created alternative systems that not only preserved individual freedoms, but also redistributed power and resources to the population.

Although the road to full freedom was still uncertain.

While the autonomous communities flourished, a sector of society remained trapped in the false promises of technocrats who still dreamed of a world under their control.

The disinformation that had been used for decades to keep the world under the control of the elites did not disappear immediately.

The global awakening was already a fact, humanity had changed forever. Cities, now governed by local democratic governments, united, and began to achieve energy autonomy and cooperation between nations.

The old power structures, based on exploitation and control, were replaced by new forms of organization.

Free technologies, driven by international cooperation, began to be deployed to eradicate the long-term effects of climate manipulation.

Humanity, which had been on the brink of extinction due to the frantic race for power, found a finally way to achieve peace, unite society and seek a better future.

Chapter 19. The Legacy of the Resistance.

As the years passed, the story of the resistance a legend. Future generations grew up with a deep understanding that power should not be concentrated in a few hands.

The legacy of those who fought to stop geoengineering and dismantle climate control lived on not only in the stories and documents they left behind, but in a world that had learned to live freely.

The rebirth of humanity had begun, and the lessons of the past would never be forgotten.

The planet was no longer the same, and would never be the same .again

In this new dawn, a world that, after overcoming the dark chapters of climate manipulation, begins a new stage of recovery and unity with infinite possibilities for the future.

Final Contribution

In this book I have tried to give voice to what many prefer to keep quiet, to what is hidden under a lethal smokescreen that crosses our skies on a daily basis.

Chemtrails, presented as a solution mitigate climate change, hide behind their official narrative a dark purpose that points directly against the life and liberty of humanity.

This is not an unsubstantiated conspiracy theory, but an urgent call to conscience and action.

The evidence is there for those who dare to look beyond what the media and governments tell us.

The effects on our health, ecosystems and the natural balance of the planet are alarming, but the silence surrounding this issue is even more chilling.

This is not just a book; it is a denunciation and an invitation not to remain passive in the face of what appears to be a covert genocide, justified in the name of a supposed common good.

If we continue to allow obscure interests to manipulate our future, we will be doomed not only as individuals, but as a species.

It is time to raise our eyes, to question what is imposed on us and to act in defense of our humanity and the Earth that shelters us.

Each of us has the power to be a beacon of truth in this sea of lies.

Change begins with the courage to open our eyes, to seek answers and to demand justice.

History will judge us by our actions, or lack thereof.

May this book be a seed for a collective awakening, because the struggle for truth is not only necessary; it is essential.

The future is in our hands.

Real images

In this series of images, taken at different times and places, I present the atmospheric phenomenon called chemtrails.

Chemtrails are responsible forthe deliberate of chemicals in the atmosphere.dispersion

Through these photos, my goal is to open a space reflection, inviting readers to explore more deeply the possible explanations behind what many of us consider an anomaly in our skies.

Image 1. Evidence of chemtrail . dispersionTheir unnatural pattern invites questions about their origin and purpose. Source: Own elaboration (2024)

Image 2. Sky saturated with multiple crisscrossing , chemtrailsforming a dense and extended pattern. Source: Own elaboration (2024)

Thin chemtrails intertwined in the sky, slowly blurring and altering the natural landscape. Source: Own elaboration (2024)

*Image 4. Sky with a thinner but equally persistent chemtrail, forming . a subtle veil covering the atmosphere*Source: Own elaboration (2024)

A chemtrail next to artificial clouds formed by the expansion of chemtrails, blurring the sky. Source: Own elaboration (2024)

Several chemtrails expanding in the sky, forming artificial clouds that hide the natural blue. Source: Own elaboration (2024)

Other information

For legal reasons, I cannot show the map with the location of the weather radars. However, I can confirm that there are several distributed throughout the national territory, and each one has a range of more than 200 km.

Printed in France by Amazon
Brétigny-sur-Orge, FR

29153145R00027